# AMERICAN ADVENTURES

★ ★ ★

## VOICES FOR FREEDOM

Slavery in America
The Underground Railroad
The 1963 Freedom March

Grateful acknowledgment is made to the following for permission to reprint previously published material:

*The Listeners* by Gloria Whelan, illustrated by Mike Benny. Text copyright © 2009 by Gloria Whelan. Illustrations copyright © 2009 by Mike Benny. Originally published by Sleeping Bear Press, 2009.

*Friend on Freedom River* by Gloria Whelan, illustrated by Gijsbert van Frankenhuyzen. Text copyright © 2004 by Gloria Whelan. Illustrations copyright © 2004 by Gijsbert van Frankenhuyzen. Originally published by Sleeping Bear Press, 2004.

*Riding to Washington* by Gwenyth Swain, illustrated by David Geister. Text copyright © 2007 by Gwenyth Swain. Illustrations copyright © 2007 by David Geister. Originally published by Sleeping Bear Press, 2007.

—◆—

## Sleeping Bear Press™

315 E. Eisenhower Parkway, Ste. 200
Ann Arbor, MI 48108
www.sleepingbearpress.com

Printed and bound in the United States.

10 9 8 7 6 5 4 3 2 1

Library of Congress Cataloging-in-Publication Data • Voices for freedom / written by Gloria Whelan, Gwenyth Swain ; • illustrated by Gijsbert van Frankenhuyzen, David Geister, Mike Benny. • pages cm. — (American adventures) • ISBN 978-1-58536-886-0 • 1. Children's stories, American. 2. Slavery—Juvenile fiction. 3. Underground Railroad—Juvenile fiction. 4. March on Washington for Jobs and Freedom (1963 : Washington, D.C.)—Juvenile fiction. 5. African Americans—History—Juvenile fiction. [1. Slavery—Fiction. 2. Underground Railroad—Fiction. 3. March on Washington for Jobs and Freedom (1963 : Washington, D.C.)—Fiction. 4. African Americans—Fiction. 5. Short stories.] • I. Whelan, Gloria, author. II. Swain, Gwenyth, 1961- author. III. Frankenhuyzen, Gijsbert van, illustrator. IV. Geister, David, illustrator. V. Benny, Mike, illustrator. • PZ5.V57 2013 • [Fic]—dc23 • 2013021845

# TABLE OF CONTENTS

# The Listeners

## SLAVERY IN AMERICA

Gloria Whelan
*Illustrated by* Mike Benny

It's still dark in the morning when the boss blows on the trumpet. We're out of bed fast.

My friends, Bobby and Sue, are too little to pick cotton like I do. Bobby drives the cows out to pasture.

Sue helps the grannies care for the babies.

We come home tired. We come home hungry, but Bobby, Sue, and me, Ella May, got more work to do after supper.

We got to listen.

Sweet potatoes in our bellies, molasses still sweet on our mouths, we're on our way. Master and Mistress at the great house don't tell us slaves nothing. We children listen and carry back the news to our parents.

The fireflies turn on and off. Bobby, Sue, and me, Ella May, hunch down in the bushes next to the great house. Listening is a job for us children. We make ourselves small as cotton seeds and quiet as shadows.

The breezes puff the curtains out the open windows. Sand flies bite us and mosquitoes stick pins in us but we don't slap at them. We're here to listen.

Master Thomas and Mistress Louise and their children, little Master John and little Mistress Grace, are enjoying the evening. Mistress Grace is playing on the piano. The music talks and talks to us and never has to say a word. We hold hands tight for fear the music's going to carry us right away.

Master Thomas tells the Mistress we slaves going to get us a new overseer to boss us. I got a smile big as an alligator's on my face. I hate the old boss. If you don't pick the cotton fast enough he comes by with his nasty cane and flicks it at you.

Bobby, Sue, and me, Ella May, hurry home fast as foxes to tell the news.

Our mammies clap hands and dance around. My daddy says, "I'm not clapping my hands until I see the new man."

The sun and me start our work at the same time. I pick with Mammy and Daddy. The

little prickers on the cotton plants bite at my fingers. We work hard in the cool of the morning. Daddy once picked four hundred pounds of cotton in one day. Nobody picks faster than my daddy does.

It's noon and time to eat. There's a big wooden bucket for us kids and clamshells for spoons. We got salt pork and corn

dumplings, and a mess of black-eyed peas looking up at us. We eat and eat until our bellies are fat as possums.

In the afternoon the sun melts me so I can hardly pick. Daddy sees my basket is nearly empty and he puts in some of his cotton. He doesn't want the boss to flick me with his nasty cane.

That night up at the great house we listen and hear Master Thomas say, "I've had an offer from the Spencers to buy William. They're short of men."

William! That's my daddy! My heart's a flock of scared birds flying every which way. I listen and listen.

"I don't believe I can spare him," Master Thomas says. "He's one of our best pickers and handy with machines. I'm thinking of teaching him how to keep the cotton gin in good repair."

I let out my breath and put my arms around Sue. Her daddy got sold away last year and she hasn't seen him since.

When I get home I hug my daddy hard and tell him the good news.

It's Saturday night. Mammy washes our clothes and near rubs the skin off us scrubbing us shiny clean for church.

We sit in the balcony. White folks sit below us in the church. When we sing "Amazing Grace" white folks and slaves sing together.

In the afternoon we go into the woods. Our church has a blue sky for the ceiling and

green grass for the floor. We've got our own preacher. He tells the story of Moses who freed the people of Israel. "The good Lord's going to free us too," he promises. "The Jubilee is coming."

We sing "All God's Children Got Wings" and "Stand Still Jordan." We sing louder than the white folks to be sure the good Lord hears us. I hope He's listening.

We're listening when the boss tells Master Thomas a plow and some horses would get the work done faster than the hoe. That sounds good to us because the hoe is hard work.

The Master says he's not buying any plow. Slaves, he says, are cheaper than horses.

Tonight every candle in the great house is lit. It looks like they hung up the sun right inside the parlor. There's a party going on. Fiddles throw music out the windows.

Bobby, Sue, and me, Ella May, dance on the grass. We dance and dance until our feet are damp with dew and the whip-poor-will says it's time to go home.

Hallelujah! The last of the cotton is picked.

I get to help Daddy be a jumper today. They hang a big bag of cotton up and we climb right in. We jump and jump on the cotton. I dance the Turkey Trot and the Mary Jane. First the cotton is soft on my toes but when we're finished dancing that bale is hard packed.

That same night when we listen we hear Mistress Louise ask, "Why don't I start a little school for the slave children?"

Master Thomas says, "What can you be thinking, my dear? It's against the law to educate slaves."

The lady who teaches Mistress Grace has given her a poem to learn. She says it over and over for her mama.

*And I will make thee beds of roses,*
*And a thousand fragrant poesies,*
*A cap of flowers, and a kirtle,*
*Embroidered all with leaves of myrtle.*

I know roses and I know myrtle bushes, but I sure don't know what a kirtle is and neither do Bobby and Sue. I say the poem all the way home and now it's my poem, too.

When I go to sleep I pretend my scratchy straw mattress is a bed of roses.

Cold weather is coming so winter clothes get handed out. Bobby's got a shirt, Sue and me got a flannel dress and drawers. No new shoes. My toes won't like that.

Master Thomas is spied walking around in his uniform, brass buttons, sword and all.

Daddy tells me, "Ella May, you and Bobby and Sue need to listen extra hard tonight. I got a feeling dangerous times are coming.

Could be our lives going to depend on what you children hear."

Master Thomas is angry. His words come out mean as rattlesnakes. "I can't believe Abraham Lincoln has been elected president," Master says. "Lincoln is a madman! He says slavery is wrong! He says slavery must end!"

Bobby, Sue, and me, Ella May, run fast.

Our mammies and daddies gather around us. This time they do the listening. We tell them, "We got us a new president. Abraham Lincoln."

Daddy says, "Moses is come! We're going to be free like the children of Israel. It's the Jubilee for sure!"

I ask Daddy, "Is our listening over?"

Daddy says, "We see the road, but we don't see all the way to where the ending is. We got to know how long is that road and how we get down it. Bobby, Sue, and you, Ella May, your listening is just begun."

## FROM THE AUTHOR,
### Gloria Whelan

The lives of slaves depended on circumstances beyond their control. They had nothing to say about whom they would work for or where they would live. They never knew when they might be separated from their children or their spouses. Hoping to learn their fate, they sent small children to hide near the windows of their masters' homes to listen.

Authors are listeners, too, that's how they find their stories. They listen. Sometimes they hear stories from people who have lived them. Sometimes they hear words spoken long ago and set down in books. It's what writers do; they listen, and like Bobby, Sue, and Ella May they pass the stories along.

# Friend on
# Freedom River

## THE UNDERGROUND RAILROAD

Gloria Whelan

*Illustrated by* Gijsbert van Frankenhuyzen

Louis watched the last of the mallard ducks lift off. Soon ice would seal the Detroit River. He turned over the fishing boat to protect it from the snows. It was what his father had always done. His father had gone north for the winter to work in the logging camps.

Before his father left he told Louis, "Son, you'll be in charge of the farm. If you don't know what to do, just do what you think I would have done."

The icy December wind shook the willow boughs and stripped the leaves from the pear trees. Louis's grandparents had brought the pear trees with them when they came from France to America. Downstream in Detroit the steamboats and schooners were racing winter to the sea.

There was a rustle in the alder bushes.

Louis thought, *A deer or a fox.*

A voice whispered, "Are you a friend?"

Louis was so startled he dropped the boat. Those words meant only one thing: runaway slaves.

He answered with the words his father had taught him long ago, words that were a sign to the slaves that they had found friends.

"What do you seek?"
"Freedom."
"Have you got faith?"
"I have hope."

A black woman wrapped in a tatter of a shawl stepped from the bushes. A small girl clung to her. A little apart stood a boy, Louis's age, 12 or 13 years old.

"God bless you," the woman said. "I'm Sarah, my girl is Lucy, and my boy is Tyler. They told us at the Baptist church in Detroit your daddy would help us. The slave catchers from Kentucky are on our trail like blood-hounds. We got to hurry across this river to Canada where a slave is free forever."

Louis knew how upset his mother would be about his trying to cross the river on a night like this. His mother had begged his father to stop carrying slaves across the river. She had warned, "The new Fugitive Slave Law means jail for anyone helping slaves escape."

Over and over his father had taken the chance, asking, "How can I see some soul sent back to slavery?"

"My father isn't here," Louis said. "There's ice on the river and the wind is strong. It's a three hour pull."

"No water's too cold and no wind is too strong for us, child," Sarah said. "We already crossed two rivers, but the Detroit River is freedom's river. It's our last chance. Our master sold away these children's daddy. They were going to sell away Tyler just like he was no different from a horse or a cow. If you don't take us, we might as well jump in and drown ourselves."

The boy was scowling at Louis. "I bet I could row that boat across the river," he said.

The boy's challenge stung Louis. "No, you couldn't," Louis said. "You got to know the currents and the shoals."

The woman was shivering. The little girl was crying without making a sound. Louis thought, *She had to learn how to cry so no one could hear her.*

Louis knew what his father would do.

"Wait here," he said.

The heat from the farmhouse kitchen wrapped around Louis like a warm coat. A kettle hung over the glowing coals. He sniffed the smell of his favorite whitefish stew. Louis had caught the whitefish himself.

"Supper is nearly ready, Louis," his mother said.

"I'll be done with the boat in a minute, Mama. I just want to get a scarf."

In the cubbyhole that was his bedroom Louis opened the window and threw out the quilt from his bed, along with a sweater and a jacket.

Then he returned to the kitchen.

Singing at the top of his voice, Louis danced his mother around the table.

> *Alouette, gentille alouette,*
> *Alouette, je te plumerai*
> *je te plumerai la tête,*
> *et la tête*
> *Alouette*

While she was laughing and dizzy from the dance, he sneaked some pain au chocolat she had set out to cool.

At the door he turned to her. "Don't worry, Mama, if it takes me a while. Darkness is just daylight turned inside out."

She smiled at him, "That's just what your father always says."

Louis gave the warm clothes, the quilt, and the chocolate bread to Sarah and her children. The boy looked like he wasn't going to put the jacket on, then he did.

"Don't mind my boy, he's stubborn," Sarah said. "I tell him there are good white people. Plenty of them helped us along our way."

Together the two boys pushed the skiff into the water, breaking a thin skin of ice. They held the boat steady while Sarah and Lucy climbed in.

"You sure you can row a boat?" Louis asked Tyler.

"I'm sure. I rowed the boat for Master Harmon when he went cat fishing. I rowed him all over Mud Lake."

Louis and Tyler slipped the oars into the locks. Like a hand reaching up out of the water the strong current grabbed hold of the skiff. The river that was such a friend to Louis in the daytime was a dangerous stranger at night.

"To fight the current we got to paddle upstream as we paddle across," Louis said. The icy wind stung their faces. The light from the farmhouse faded.

"How did you get here?" Louis asked Sarah.

"We crossed the Ohio River and come station to station on the Underground Railroad."

"We followed the North Star," Lucy said.

"They sent big dogs sniffing and growling after us," Tyler said.

Sarah said, "There were kind folk took us in, hungry, and sent us off full."

The boat shuddered as it plowed through the thin ice. In the daytime Louis had the gulls and the other fishermen to keep him company, but in the winter night it seemed to Louis the four of them were the only people left on earth. Louis's teeth were chattering and his fingers were numb. Sarah held Lucy close to protect her from the wind.

The light from the farmhouse had long since disappeared but now another light shone on the river. It was the lantern of a patrol boat. Louis felt as if he had swallowed a piece of the ice. If they were discovered, Louis would be sent to jail. Sarah and her children would be sent back to slavery.

"Stop rowing," Louis whispered to Tyler. "We got to be quiet."

As soon as they stopped rowing, their boat began drifting away from Canada. The voices of the men carried across the water as the patrol boat swept by. The wake from the patrol boat splashed against the skiff, but the boat's lantern didn't catch them.

When the patrol boat was out of hearing the boys began to row again. Their arms

ached from trying to make up the distance they had lost.

Tyler was as worried as Louis. To break the silence he asked, "What kind of fish you catch in this river?"

"Whitefish, herring, perch, sturgeon. My papa caught a sturgeon that weighed 80 pounds."

"That's a big fish. You got to be strong to catch it. You got to be smart to catch a catfish. The best thing is just to put on a heavy sinker and let some crawlers bump along the bottom of the lake."

The wind was against them and the ice was thickening. For every foot they gained, the boat seemed to slip back a foot into the black water. Louis had never been so cold.

He wished he could ask his papa if he had done the right thing to risk their lives.

Sarah began to sing and the children joined her.

*O Lord, O my Lord, keep me from sinkin' down*
*I tell you what I mean to do*
*Keep me from sinkin' down*
*Sometimes I'm up, sometimes I'm down*
*Keep me from sinkin' down*
*Sometimes I'm almost on the ground*
*Keep me from sinkin' down*
*I look up yonder and what do I see?*
*I see the angels beckonin' me*
*Keep me from sinkin' down*

After a minute Louis sang, too. The wind tossed the words back at them and they sent them back into the wind.

They all saw the light at the same time.

"That another patrol boat?" Tyler whispered.

But the light stayed still.

"That's Canada!" Louis shouted.

He and Tyler pulled on the oars. They jumped out and dragged the skiff onto the shore.

Louis pounded on the door of a nearby farmhouse. He held his breath. What if they were turned away?

A startled man and woman hurried them inside. When everyone was warmed and fed, they urged Louis to stay.

"You can't go back tonight," the man said.

"I have to. Mama will know the boat's gone. If I don't come back she'll think I drowned for sure."

Sarah threw her arms around Louis. Lucy hugged his leg. The two boys shook hands. "I'll come over this summer and we'll get us a sturgeon," Louis promised.

Then Louis left them to their new freedom.

The cold wind stung his face. Over and over Louis had to break the ice with his paddle. His hands were so cold he could hardly hold the oars. The boat was lighter now and easier to row. It was also a lot easier to be afraid when you were alone. He wished Tyler were there.

To keep himself company he began to sing, *Keep me from sinkin' down*. He could almost hear Sarah and her children joining in.

On the distant shore a light broke into the darkness. This time it was his name that came to him on the wind. He dug the oars into the water, pushing aside the ice.

His mother was waiting on the shore. Her arms were around him.

He told her about Sarah and Lucy and Tyler.

"When Papa comes back," Louis said, "I'll tell him, 'Papa, I did what I thought you would do.'"

## FROM THE AUTHOR,
Gloria Whelan

It is estimated that 40,000 slaves traveled Michigan's Underground Railroad. For many of the slaves the road to freedom led through Detroit and across the Detroit River to Canada.

To commemorate those perilous journeys a "Gateway to Freedom" monument stands on Detroit's Hart Plaza Riverfront Promenade. The 12-foot bronze monument depicts eight figures looking across the Detroit River to Windsor, Ontario, in Canada.

Across the Detroit River on the Windsor Civic Esplanade, the 22-foot "Tower of Freedom" monument, with its bronze "Flame of Freedom," celebrates Canada's proud part in the Underground Railroad.

# Riding to
# Washington

## THE 1963 FREEDOM MARCH

Gwenyth Swain
*Illustrated by* David Geister

I know why they're putting me on that bus to Washington. It's because I get in trouble.

"Trouble with a capital T," Mama always says. Most times she says it with a smile in her eyes. Other times, like when I slam the screen door by accident and wake up the twins—well, those times I have to look hard to find the smile.

Daddy doesn't want me to go with him on that bus to Washington, but it sounds like I'm going anyhow.

"A whole lot of people are going to hear Dr. King speak," he told Mama one night late when he thought I was sleeping. "I don't like the idea of taking Janie. She's a spitfire."

You know what spitfire means? I think it must mean I spit fire. Guess that's Daddy's way of saying I'm trouble.

"Honey," Mama told Daddy, "that girl makes more trouble than I can bear, what with the twins teething."

So, that's how I ended up riding to Washington, hundreds of miles from home. I knew why I was going, but I wasn't so sure why Daddy was.

We don't have coloreds, or black folks, living in our part of Indianapolis. I don't see many at all, except on TV. Blacks on TV live mostly in the South. They get sprayed at with fire hoses and nipped at by police dogs. But Daddy knows a whole lot of coloreds here from work.

I think that's why Daddy's going to Washington to hear Dr. Martin Luther King speak. Because he thinks we should all work together. But Daddy just says, "We'll see history, Janie. History."

I study history at school, and believe you me it's not exciting. Neither was leaving Indianapolis.

On Tuesday, at the Walker Theatre downtown, a bunch of old buses waited for us. They had names on them like Crispus Attucks School and Rollins Grove AME Church. And everyone getting onto them

was dressed like it was the first day of school or Easter Sunday. I figured I was in trouble again, wearing my favorite overalls, but Paul Taylor, from Daddy's painting crew, smiled at me.

"Nice to meet you," said his wife. She had a hat like Mrs. Kennedy wears and a suit to match. "Your overalls look comfy," she said,

winking. She was right.

There were old people mixed with young people. Preachers mixed with farmers. And me and Daddy and just a few other whites mixed in with a whole bunch of coloreds. More than I'd ever seen in one place.

I was glad when it was finally time to get on the bus.

I pressed close to Daddy, even in the heat.

We all brought picnic lunches, but by night-time, we were hungry again. We stopped one, two, three times. Each time Paul Taylor and the driver went inside a restaurant. And each time they came back, shaking their heads.

"No service for mixed crowds," Paul explained.

"Why can't we go in?" I whispered to Daddy. "You and me aren't mixed."

"Would you want to eat where others can't?"

I was so hungry I'd have eaten almost anything, almost anywhere. But maybe Daddy was right. Maybe it was best to stick together. Still, I wondered about the coloreds. They didn't act like troublemakers—and I know a lot about trouble.

To keep our minds off food, Paul Taylor started singing. I stumbled and fumbled over words everyone else seemed to know:

*This little light of mine, I'm gonna let it shine.*
*This little light of mine, I'm gonna let it shine...*

We drove across farm fields and through cities, over rivers and mountains. The roll of the wheels put me to sleep until we lurched to a stop. We were at a gas station. Daddy's watch said it was nearly midnight.

Mrs. Taylor walked to the front to ask the
driver a question. I only heard his answer.
"No, Ma'am," he told her. "I can't let you
off here."

She stared at the sign over the restroom door. "No Coloreds" it read. She sniffed in disgust. "I'm going," she said.

Her voice made me rise to my feet. Suddenly, I needed to go, too.

"Sir," I told the driver, "I got to go."

"You could be getting yourself into trouble, young lady," the driver warned.

"I got to go!" I said.

Mrs. Taylor and I walked arm in arm into the station, where a skinny boy not much older than me was trying to stay awake behind a counter. "Young man," Mrs. Taylor said, "we would like the key to the ladies' room, please."

Her voice was so strong and clear it woke that boy right up. He looked at one of us, then the other.

"I . . . I can't let you in there," he told Mrs. Taylor. Her arm stiffened in mine.

"Yes, you can," I said.

They both looked down at me, startled.

"Sure," I went on. "It's like my mama and daddy always say, 'You got the choice to do the right thing or not.' " (I didn't say that they usually told me that right after I'd gotten into trouble.)

The boy blinked, confused.

I kept on, like I was talking to a friend. "Mama says I make a lot of wrong choices, but I think letting us in would be the right one now."

The boy's cheeks flushed red. He coughed. Then he looked the other way and shoved the key across the counter, like he'd mislaid it—right in plain sight.

In the bathroom, there was a machine with a long towel looping out of it.

I reached up to yank on it as hard as I could to see how much towel was inside, but I stopped short. Mrs. Taylor gave me a look while she straightened her hat.

When we took the key back, our thank-yous overlapped. The boy tried to look busy. He didn't have a "you're welcome" to spare for us.

Mr. Taylor was singing as we pulled back onto the road:

*Get on board, children, children!*
*Get on board, children, children!*
*Get on board, children, children!*
*Let's fight for human rights!*

This time, the words made sense and I sang along.

It was just getting light when we finally parked in a field. Never in my life had I seen so many buses. It was like the biggest basketball tourney you could imagine, only we were all rooting for the same team.

"Morning," Mrs. Taylor called to me as we left the bus.

"Fine weather," Daddy said to no one in particular.

None of us looked like we'd been riding on a bus for a day and a night. We all looked as if we'd just woken up to a day we'd been dreaming about.

Later, when Dr. King was speaking, we all stood together in a group. We were miles away from the podium, but would you believe it? I was sure he was looking right at me.

Dr. King's speech sounded fine. The way he said it was just like music. But I wondered to myself: Why is he telling me about his

dream? What's it got to do with me?

Then I felt a hand resting soft on my shoulder. Mrs. Taylor gazed at me, tears streaming down her face. And that's when I knew it: that the dream belonged not just to Dr. King and Mrs. Taylor and her husband, but to me and Daddy, and maybe even to that boy at the gas station, too.

## FROM THE AUTHOR,
### Gwenyth Swain

The buses began arriving just after daybreak on August 28, 1963. They parked in long lines, bumper nudging bumper, windows cracked open to let in a breeze. It was going to be a hot, muggy day. The thousands of people who got off the buses weren't too concerned about the heat. Even though many hadn't slept much the night before, they weren't especially tired. The way my father remembers it, the mood was festive, and "there was a feeling of peace."

My father and grandfather, both white men from south-central Indiana, rode the bus to Washington to hear Dr. Martin Luther King Jr. and others speak on that August day. I was only two years old at the time, but I have long wondered what it might have been like to be a child at the great March on Washington.

In the history books, the March on Washington is best remembered for Martin Luther King Jr.'s historic "I Have a Dream" speech. But those who arrived by bus had already made history before King stood before the crowd of over 200,000 at the Lincoln Memorial. The moment they boarded buses in Indianapolis, Memphis, Chicago, and other cities across the country, these people— black and white, Christian, Muslim, and Jew—had begun to realize a dream of coming together in peace. And on that morning in Washington, D.C., they and their dream arrived.

A poet and author of many award-winning children's books, **Gloria Whelan** received the National Book Award for her young adult novel, *Homeless Bird*. Her books include *Yuki and the One Thousand Carriers* and *Yatandou*. Ms. Whelan lives near Lake St. Clair in Michigan.

**Gwenyth Swain** enjoys weaving family stories and historical events together in fiction. Her books include *Hope & Tears: Ellis Island Voices, Chig and the Second Spread*, and *I Wonder As I Wander*. She lives in St. Paul, Minnesota.

**Gijsbert van Frankenhuyzen** has illustrated more than 20 picture books for Sleeping Bear Press. His books include *T is for Titanic: A Titanic Alphabet*, *Mackinac Bridge: The Five-Mile Poem*, and the best-selling *The Legend of Sleeping Bear*. He lives in Bath, Michigan.

**David Geister**'s deep appreciation for the drama of American history and the desire to tell those stories inspires his artwork. His books include *B is for Battle Cry: A Civil War Alphabet* and *Surviving the Hindenburg*. He lives in Minneapolis, Minnesota.

**Mike Benny**'s illustrations have appeared in *Time*, *The New Yorker*, and *Sports Illustrated* magazines. His awards include three gold and two silver medals from the Society of Illustrators. Mike lives in Austin, Texas.